ART ATTACKS!

CHAD SELL

ALFRED A. KNOPF NEW YORK

THIS IS A BORZOI BOOK PUBLISHED BY ALFRED A. KNOPF

This is a work of fiction. Names, characters, places, and incidents either are the product of the author's imagination or are used fictitiously. Any resemblance to actual persons, living or dead, events, or locales is entirely coincidental. Except for the Art Institute of Chicago and Stan's Donuts. Those are real places. They just don't (usually) have doodles causing mischief in them.

Visit us on the Web! rhcbooks.com

Educators and librarians, for a variety of teaching tools, visit us at RHTeachersLibrarians.com

Library of Congress Cataloging-in-Publication Data is available upon request.
ISBN 978-1-9848-9473-1 (trade) – ISBN 978-0-593-56930-6 (lib. bdg.) –
ISBN 978-1-9848-9475-5 (ebook)

The text of this book is set in Creative Block BB.
The illustrations were created using Clip Studio Paint.
Interior design by Chad Sell

MANUFACTURED IN CHINA
10 9 8 7 6 5 4 3 2 1

First Edition

This book is dedicated to everyone at the
Art Institute of Chicago. Thank you for inspiring me
endlessly with your world-class collection of art.
Sorry for wrecking it.
—C.S.

ART CLUB

DREW

HER CHARACTER, LEVI THE LEVIATHAN

AND HER DOODLES!

HER CHARACTER, DINAH DARE, INVENTOR EXTRAORDINAIRE

BECK

AMEER

HIS CHARACTER, CAPTAIN COCKATOO

HER CHARACTERS,
THE MAGICAL BUTTERFLY
BOYFRIENDS

TJ

THEIR CHARACTER,
BRU THE WITCH

MR. SCHNEIDER,
ART TEACHER

SO, UMM...
THIS BABY?
HE'S FROM A PAINTING.
AT...THE ART INSTITUTE OF CHICAGO.
HE IS **NOT** SUPPOSED TO BE HERE.
I SORT OF... ACCIDENTALLY... **KIDNAPPED** HIM?
3

AND SO...
I WAS HOPING...
MAYBE...
THAT YOU COULD HELP ME **SNEAK HIM BACK** INTO THE INSTITUTE?

UM...

HOW DO YOU ACCIDENTALLY KIDNAP A BABY FROM A PAINTING?

REMEMBER HOW MIKE LIKES HATS?
HE STOLE THE BABY'S HAT A WHILE AGO, AND I WAS TRYING TO GIVE IT BACK.
I SENT LEVI IN WITH IT...
AND INSTEAD OF LEAVING THE HAT...
HE CAME BACK WITH THE BABY.

SO... THE FACT THAT NONE OF YOUR DOODLES EVER DO WHAT THEY'RE SUPPOSED TO DO IS WHY WE'RE IN THIS MESS?
THAT'S NOT FAIR, TJ.

HEY, I LOVE NONCONFORMISTS.
AND ALSO MESSES.
THAT EXPLAINS A LOT.

HOW CAN WE **HELP**, DREW?
WITH THE **HEIST**?
IT'S MORE LIKE A **REVERSE** HEIST, RIGHT?
SNEAKING SOMETHING BACK **IN**?
STILL COOL.

HERE'S THE THING.
I...CAN'T ACTUALLY GO **INTO** THE ART INSTITUTE.
THERE'S THIS MEAN OLD LADY THERE WHO'S... MEAN?
SHE'S ON THE BOARD OF DIRECTORS OR SOMETHING.
AND SHE **KNOWS** I HAD SOMETHING TO DO WITH ALL THIS.

SO...SHE'S LIKE YOUR **NEMESIS**?
YOU HAVE A **NEMESIS**, DREW!
I WANT A NEMESIS.

SO YOU NEED **US** TO GET THE BABY INTO THE INSTITUTE?
DOES THE BABY **WANT** TO GO BACK?

WELL, HE **LOVES** LEVI...
BUT HIS **MOM** MUST **MISS** HIM, RIGHT?
HE BELONGS AT THE INSTITUTE.

DREW, WE'LL NEED AN ADULT TO TAKE US DOWNTOWN.
DO YOU HAVE ANYONE IN MIND?

HEY, KIDDOS!
BECAUSE--
ANYBODY HUNGRY?
DAD!!!
THIS IS A **PRIVATE MEETING**!
WE'RE TALKING ABOUT, UH, SECRET ART CLUB STUFF!

CHAPTER 1: SECRET ART CLUB STUFF

SHALL WE HEAD IN, KIDS?
I KNOW HOW EAGER YOU WERE TO COME BACK HERE!
WE JUST NEED A SECOND, MR. SCHNEIDER.
WHAT ARE YOU WHISPERING ABOUT OVER THERE?
IS SOMETHING GOING ON?
OH, WE WERE... JUST WONDERING IF WE COULD GO TO STAN'S FOR DONUTS LATER?
WELL, PERHAPS!
THOUGH THE INSTITUTE HAS A LOVELY CAFÉ, TOO.
REALLY? DO THEY HAVE DONUTS?
HUH, I'M NOT SURE...
OKAY, ARE WE ALL SET?
I WANT TO GO OVER THE PLAN AGAIN.

ONCE WE MAKE IT TO THE PAINTING, WE'LL TEXT YOU.
LEVI WILL BRING THE BABY AND DROP HIM OFF AT OUR L STOP.
AND YOU KNOW HOW TO GET THERE?
I'VE MEMORIZED EVERY FLOOR OF THE MUSEUM.
WE KNOW THE PLAN, DREW.
BUT DOES **LEVI**?
HE DOESN'T **LIKE** IT, BUT HE KNOWS WHAT HE HAS TO DO.

MOMENTS LATER...
WHAT? DREW, YOU WANT TO STAY OUT **HERE**?

THIS ALL SEEMS VERY **STRANGE**.
STRANGE?

I DON'T KNOW WHAT YOU COULD **POSSIBLY** BE TALKING ABOUT.

IS SOMETHING **WRONG**?
YOU CAN **TALK** TO ME, DREW.
NOTHING'S WRONG, I--
BZZT

IS THAT...?
WE'RE IN! SEND LEVI!

OKAY, LEVI, GO!
THAT'S...

THE BABY!
THE MISSING BABY!!!
WHY DO YOU HAVE THE BABY?!

IT WAS AN ACCIDENT!
WE'RE TRYING TO GET HIM BACK TO HIS MOM!
OH DEAR. OOOOH DEAR.
WHY DIDN'T YOU TELL ME, DREW?!
YOU KNOW I WOULD DO ANYTHING FOR YOU KIDS!
I... BZZT
IT...
UH... BZZT
BZZT
ART CLUB
DREW!!!!
EMERGENCY!!!!
HELP!!!!

DREW!
WHAT--?

HUH?

WAS THAT...?
CALL MRS. KRONG!

WHAT'S GOING ON?!

IT'S THE BABY'S **MOM**!
SHE'S **MAD**! LEVI'S **SCARED** OF HER!

UH-OH.

LEVI!
ANGRY MOMMA!
CALM DOWN!!!

YOU HAVE EVERY REASON TO BE ANGRY WITH LEVI. AND ME.
BUT WE'RE HERE TO GIVE YOUR BABY BACK.

AND, LEVI, I KNOW YOU LIKE THE BABY VERY MUCH...
AND YOU'LL MISS HIM A LOT, BUT...
IT'S TIME TO GIVE HIM BACK.

OKAY?

STOP!!!

STOP THAT GIRL!
AND HER MONSTER!
SCRUB IT OFF THE WALLS!

IS THAT **HER**?!
THE MEAN OLD...?
IT'S **HER**!!
SHE'S TERRIFYING!

LEVI! **RUN**!
RUN!!!

IN A NEARBY GALLERY...
DREW?!
WHERE DID SHE GO?

OH!
LEVI!
WHAT...

...IN THE WORLD...

...IS GOING ON?!

CRASH!
WHAT WAS THAT?

UH-OH.

LEVI! WE HAVE TO GET OUT OF HERE!

??

EEE!

GRAB!
AAA!

LEVI!!
THAT GUY'S ATTACKING LEVI!

BUT-- HE DIDN'T--
QUICK! GET YOUR CHARACTERS!
ALREADY ON IT!

ART CLUB, UNITE!

THIS IS AN **OUTRAGE**!
WHAT ARE YOU CHILDREN **DOING**?!
GRRR
!!!!!!!
GUARDS! **STOP** THIS!
ALL OF THIS!!
HOW?!
WHAT'S EVEN **HAPPENING**?!
OH. MY. WORD.

THE BABY'S BACK WITH HIS MOM, SO, UH...

MISSION ACCOMPLISHED!

WE NEED TO GET **OUT** OF HERE!

COME ON, CAP!

MEET ME AT HOME, LEVI!

BUT...
BUT WAIT!

YOU--
YOU'RE NOT GETTING AWAY WITH THIS!!!

CHAPTER 2: MISSION... ACCOMPLISHED?

I, UM, GOT US A LOT.
THANKS, AMEER.
YEAH.
SO...THAT WAS BAD, RIGHT?
DISASTROUS.
GUYS?
ZEN!!!
WHAT HAPPENED?
WHERE WERE YOU?

I, UH, HAD TO TAKE CARE OF SOMETHING.
HUH?!

LEVI **BIT** THAT MAN.
HIS HAND WAS HURT.

SO? HE DESERVED IT. THAT GUY'S A **MONSTER**.
YEAH, BUT **LEVI'S** THE ONE WHO BROKE HIS STATUE. **THAT'S** WHY HE WAS SO ANGRY.
ZEN, WHAT DID YOU **DO**?

I DREW HIM A **BANDAGE**.
I HOPE HIS HAND FEELS BETTER.

YOU **HELPED** HIM?!
OF COURSE I HELPED HIM!

WHAT ABOUT MR. SCHNEIDER?
IS HE MEETING US HERE?

HE STAYED BEHIND.
TO TRY AND EXPLAIN.

HE **WHAT**?!
HE DIDN'T EVEN **KNOW** ANYTHING!
THIS WASN'T HIS **FAULT**!

WE GOT THE BABY BACK TO HIS MOM!
MISSION ACCOMPLISHED!
SO...THERE'S NOTHING TO WORRY ABOUT!

...RIGHT?

AT THE ART INSTITUTE...

BARRY, LOOK!

HE'S TRYING TO PUT HIS STATUE BACK TOGETHER.

YOU SHOULD LET **US** HANDLE THAT, DORIAN.

I'LL ADD IT TO OUR LIST OF THINGS TO FIX.

WAIT. WHAT'S ON HIS HAND?

DID SOMEONE **DRAW** ON DORIAN GRAY?

IT'S... A BANDAGE!

WITH... A LITTLE **HEART**?

WE'VE GOT **A LOT** OF WORK TO DO. I HOPE YOU DIDN'T HAVE PLANS TONIGHT!

JUST ANOTHER ALL-NIGHTER WITH **YOU**!

HA HA!

HEY, DREW!
ARE YOU HUNGRY?
ARE YOU... **OKAY**?
DID SOMETHING **HAPPEN** ON YOUR FIELD TRIP?

I...
I SHOULD HAVE TOLD YOU SOONER.
SEE, A FEW DAYS AGO...
DREW?
THAT WAS YOUR **ART TEACHER**.
WHAT?!

MR. SCHNEIDER TOLD ME WHAT HAPPENED AT THE INSTITUTE.
BUT...
WHAT HAPPENED TO HIM?!
IS HE...?
HE'S BEEN PUT ON LEAVE, DREW.
WHAT...?
WHAT DOES THAT MEAN?
HE WON'T BE BACK AT SCHOOL UNTIL THINGS GET SORTED OUT.
IT SOUNDS... SERIOUS.

LATER THAT NIGHT...
DID YOU HEAR??????
IT'S NOT FAIR!
WE HAVE TO FIGHT THIS!!

IT'S TOTAL %$&#
LET'S TAKE DOWN THE ART INSTITUTE.

NOT PRODUCTIVE, TJ.
WE NEED A PLAN.
FIND A LAYWER??
LAWYER.
PETITION SCHOOL BOARD??
REGROUP IN MORNING WITH IDEAS??

WE'LL FIGURE IT OUT!!!
SEE YOU TOMORROW!!!!
ART CLUB UNITED!!!!

AT THE ART INSTITUTE...
ZZZ

CHAPTER 3: WHAT HAPPENED

MORNING, DOODLES.
DID YOU SLEEP OKAY?
I DIDN'T.
HAVE YOU SEEN LEVI?
DID HE EVER COME HOME LAST NIGHT?
COULD HE STILL BE AT THE ART INSTITUTE?
DID... SOMETHING **HAPPEN**?

OH, HERE, PILE UP YOUR SLEEPING BAGS!

I'LL GET THEM OUT OF YOUR WAY.

I'VE GOT TO DRAW YOU BETTER BEDS AND STUFF SOON.

I'M SORRY IT'S TAKING SO LONG.

WHERE HAVE YOU BEEN?
ARE YOU **OKAY**?
I WAS **WORRIED**!
I TOLD YOU TO COME RIGHT BACK HERE!
IF SOMETHING **HAPPENED** TO YOU, I...
BUT, HEY, IT'S FINE!
YOU'RE FINE.
I'M JUST GLAD YOU'RE BACK!
NOW.
WHO'S HUNGRY?

GOOD MORNING, DREW!
OH! HEY, RICKY!
HEY, ERNESTO!

WHAT WOULD YOU LIKE TO EAT, SWEETHEART?
WHAT'S THE **SPECIAL**?
BLUEBERRY PANCAKE PLATTER.
OOH, I'LL HAVE **THAT**.

WHAT'S THE SPECIAL TODAY AT YOUR **DOODLE DINER,** RICKY?
SLIME SOUP WITH MARSHMALLOWS!

DO YOU HAVE ENOUGH FOR LEVI?
SURE!
HE ALREADY HAD SOME LAST NIGHT!
HUH? LAST NIGHT?
HOW ARE YOU FEELING, DREW?
AFTER EVERYTHING THAT HAPPENED?
OH.
I MEAN, TERRIBLE.
IT WAS PRETTY MUCH ALL MY FAULT.
LIKE USUAL.
THE LAST PERSON WHO SHOULD GET IN TROUBLE IS...
MR. SCHNEIDER?!

I'M SO SORRY
ARE YOU OKAY
I FEEL TERRIBLE
AND NOW

MR. SCHNEIDER!!
GONNA DO
EVERYTHING
I CAN TO FIX
THINGS AN

YOU'RE
SUCH A GOOD
TEACHER AND
I LOVE ART
CLUB
HAVE TO
COME BACK
TO SCHOOL
AND
WHAT IF YOU
GO TO JAIL AND
NEVER GET OUT
WILL
WE CAN
FIX THIS AND
MAYBE EXPLAIN
EVERYTHING

I CAME TO TELL YOU NOT TO WORRY, KIDS.
EVERYTHING WILL BE **FINE**, YOU'LL SEE.
BUT...
IT'S **OUR** FAULT THAT--
YOU SHOULDN'T BLAME YOURSELVES FOR **ANY** OF THIS.
IT WILL ALL SORT ITSELF OUT.
AND MAYBE I'LL BE BACK IN SCHOOL BY MONDAY!
I HOPE SO, MR. SCHNEIDER!
STAY OUT OF TROUBLE, AND...
SEE YOU **SOON**!
MOMENTS LATER...
OKAY, SO, **REALLY**...
HOW ARE WE GOING TO FIX THIS?

CAN WE REACH OUT TO THE ART INSTITUTE?
TRY TO **EXPLAIN** WHAT HAPPENED?
THEY **HAVE** TO BE REASONABLE...
WHO? THE MEAN OLD LADY?
YOU THINK **SHE'S** GONNA GO EASY ON MR. SCHNEIDER?
YEAH, SHE LITERALLY SHOWED UP IN MY DREAMS LAST NIGHT.
AND NOT FOR THE FIRST TIME, EITHER.
SHE'S ALWAYS **CHASING** ME.
"YOU ARE **NOT** GOING TO GET AWAY WITH THIS!!!!"
"THERE IS **NO ESCAPE,** FOOLISH CHILDREN!"
HA HA!
UH...

AHHHH!!!!
WHERE IS HE?
WHAT? I...HOW...? WHO?!
WITH THE RIDICULOUS HAT!
JOHN NICHOLSON, JR.
THE BABY!

RARRGHHHH!!
ARE
YOU
KIDDING ME?!?!
WE BROUGHT HIM BACK!
MISSION ACCOMPLISHED!!
PROBLEM SOLVED!

SADLY NOT. BECAUSE HE DISAPPEARED AGAIN IN THE MIDDLE OF THE NIGHT.

I'M HERE TO GET HIM BACK.

NONE OF US HAD ANYTHING TO DO WITH HIM GOING MISSING... THIS TIME.
YEAH, STOP COMING FOR US, SCARY LADY!
MY NAME IS CORNELIA KRONG.
AND I'M THAD!
YES, THIS IS MY GRANDSON, THAD KRONG.
THE KRONG NAME MAY BE FAMILIAR TO SOME OF YOU...
SINCE IT IS THE KRONG WING OF AMERICAN ART THAT NOW STANDS ON THE BRINK OF DESTRUCTION BECAUSE OF YOU CHILDREN.

MRS. KRONG, YOU CAN'T JUST COME IN HERE AND ACCUSE MY DAUGHTER OF, UH...
DESTROYING THE ART INSTITUTE...?
HOW COULD SHE EVEN DO THAT?
I'LL EXPLAIN EVERYTHING TO THEM...
ON OUR WAY TO THE INSTITUTE.
US?!
BECAUSE I FEAR THAT THESE CHILDREN... ARE OUR ONLY HOPE OF SAVING IT.
YES, WELL...
IT WAS THAD'S IDEA.
HE'S A VERY THOUGHTFUL YOUNG MAN.
BLAAGHHH!!!

WE'LL ONLY HELP YOU ON ONE CONDITION.

WHAT'S THAT?

YOU LET OUR ART TEACHER OFF THE HOOK.

THAT MAN IS RESPONSIBLE FOR THE LOSS AND DESTRUCTION OF **PRICELESS** INSTITUTE PROPERTY!

HE **WILL** BE HELD TO ACCOUNT!

HE HAD NOTHING TO DO WITH IT.

HE DIDN'T EVEN KNOW WHY WE WERE REALLY THERE.

IT'S OUT OF THE QUESTION!

THEN WE'RE **NOT COMING**.

I WILL NOT BACK DOWN TO A CHILD!
DO YOU EVEN KNOW WHO I AM?!
YEAH, CORNELIA KRONG.
I--
YOU LITERALLY JUST TOLD US.
OKAY. WE'LL DROP THE CHARGES.
BUT ONLY IF YOU CAN FIX THIS MESS.
FINE.
GOOD.

OUTSIDE THE DINER...
DREW, YOU DON'T **HAVE** TO GO WITH THE SCARY LADY.
IN FACT, MAYBE YOU **SHOULDN'T**.
IT'S OKAY, DAD.
I WANT TO MAKE THIS **RIGHT**.
HOWEVER I CAN.
BUT...
DON'T WORRY.
THEY'LL BE SAFE IN MY CARE.
I'M NOT A **MONSTER**.
I'M NOT **ENTIRELY** CONVINCED OF THAT.

SOON AFTER...
UM, SO... MRS. KRONG? CORNELIA?
I JUST CALL HER GRAMMY.
CAN YOU TELL US WHAT **HAPPENED** AT THE INSTITUTE?
AS BEST AS I CAN.
BUCKLE UP, CHILDREN.

AFTER A **GENTLE** INTERROGATION OF EVERYONE WHO WAS THERE LAST NIGHT...
I'VE PIECED TOGETHER A BASIC UNDERSTANDING OF WHAT HAPPENED.

HANNAH, THE CHILD'S MOTHER, WOKE UP TO FIND JUNIOR GONE. **AGAIN**.

UNDERSTANDABLY, SHE WAS **QUITE** UPSET, AND SHE WENT LOOKING FOR HIM.

THE ONLY SIGN OF HIM WAS A FEATHER THAT HAD FALLEN FROM HIS HAT.
IT WAS NEAR THE PORTRAIT OF DORIAN GRAY...
WHICH WAS SUSPICIOUSLY **EMPTY**.

NATURALLY, SHE ASSUMED THE WORST:
DORIAN HAD TAKEN HER CHILD.
NEEDLESS TO SAY, HANNAH WAS FURIOUS.
SHE TOOK OUT HER ANGER ON DORIAN'S PRIZED POSSESSION: HIS CAT STATUE.
WHEN DORIAN RETURNED LATER, HE FOUND ONLY TINY, SHATTERED PIECES OF IT.
AND AS YOU MIGHT GUESS...
HE FOLLOWED THAT TRAIL OF DESTRUCTION RIGHT BACK TO HANNAH.

THINGS DID NOT GO WELL.
EACH OF THEM HAS RALLIED OTHERS TO THEIR CAUSE...
AMASSING ALLIES FROM LIKE-MINDED PAINTINGS.
HANNAH AND HER WARRIORS OF RIGHTEOUS RAGE...

DORIAN AND HIS...
DARK ART ARMY.
THEIR ARGUMENTS AND ACCUSATIONS HAVE ESCALATED TO THE POINT OF WAR.
PAINTINGS HAVE ALREADY BEEN DAMAGED, AND IT'S ONLY GETTING WORSE.

A WHILE LATER...
GOOD MORNING, GREG. HOW IS IT IN THERE?
A **MESS**, MRS. KRONG.
EXIT
STAFF ONLY
WE NEED TO FIND THE BABY AND END THIS MADNESS.
THE DAMAGE ALREADY DONE HAS BEEN **INCALCULABLE**.

WE'VE NEVER SEEN **ANYTHING** LIKE THIS.
THIS EXHIBIT IS CLOSED

ALL THESE POOR PEOPLE...
WHERE ARE THEY **GOING**?
AS FAR AS THEY CAN, SADLY.
CORNELIA, **WAIT**.
WE'RE JUST **KIDS**.
IF **YOU** CAN'T STOP THIS, HOW CAN YOU EXPECT **US** TO?
IT'S NOT **FAIR**!
AND IT'S NOT FAIR TO MR. SCHNEIDER!
DO YOU REALLY WANT HIM TO GET **FIRED** BECAUSE OF US?
I DON'T WANT **ANY** OF THIS TO BE HAPPENING, CHILDREN.
PLEASE KNOW THAT.

WHOA...
LOOK!
BUT...
WHAT DID YOU BRING US HERE TO **DO**?
LIKE I SAID, IT WAS **THAD'S** IDEA.
WHAT WAS?
DO YOU REMEMBER WHEN YOU FIRST MET US?
WHEN YOUR DOODLES WERE RUNNING THROUGH THE INSTITUTE?
YEAH, BUT WHAT...?
ALL OF YOUR DRAWINGS!
THEY CAN FIND THE **BABY**!

YES, YOUR **DOODLES** CAN SEARCH OUR COLLECTIONS **FAR** MORE THOROUGHLY THAN WE CAN.
THEY CAN FIND WHERE DORIAN HAS HIDDEN THE BABY.
BUT WHAT IF DORIAN **DIDN'T** TAKE HIM?
OF **COURSE** HE TOOK HIM!
YEAH, HE'S LIKE A SUPERVILLAIN STRAIGHT OUT OF A COMIC BOOK.
BUT...
WHERE IS DORIAN **NOW**?
WE DON'T KNOW.
HIS FORCES HAVE SCATTERED, PRESUMABLY TO RECRUIT MORE ALLIES TO THE DARK ART ARMY.
WE SHOULD SPLIT UP AND LOOK FOR THE BABY.
IF WE FOLLOW THE DARK ART, MAYBE WE'LL FIND WHERE THEY'RE KEEPING HIM!
YEAH!

TJ, WANT TO CHECK OUT THE MODERN ART WING?
SOUNDS GOOD!
ANYTHING'S BETTER THAN THESE OLD WHITE GUYS IN **WIGS**.

DO YOU WANT TO TEAM UP, ZEN?
UM...
I DON'T WANT TO LEAVE DREW WITH...
WITH **CORNELIA**? HA HA, THANKS, BUT DON'T WORRY.

OKAY, WELL... IF YOU'RE SURE! GOOD LUCK!
THANKS!
I'LL... PROBABLY NEED IT.

MOST OF THESE PAINTINGS HAVE BEEN HERE FOR DECADES.

THEY HAVE BEEN **PERFECTLY HAPPY** STAYING **IN** THEIR FRAMES AND **OUT** OF TROUBLE.

IT'S JUST...
I TRY TO GIVE MY DOODLES LOTS OF STUFF TO DO.
OTHERWISE... THEY GET INTO TROUBLE.
TROUBLE?
THEY'VE CERTAINLY BROUGHT **PLENTY** OF IT HERE.
BUT ONCE WE FIND THE BABY, IT'LL BE OKAY, RIGHT?
ALL THE DAMAGE, CAN IT BE **FIXED**?
WE HAVE THE GREATEST ART RESTORATION DEPARTMENT IN THE WORLD...
BUT IT TAKES THEM **MONTHS** TO RESTORE A SINGLE PAINTING.
OH.
EEEE!
$ø&#!
THEN I HOPE WE FIND JUNIOR **SOON**.
BECAUSE HANNAH IS GOING TO **TEAR THIS PLACE APART** LOOKING FOR HIM.

I FEEL **AWFUL** ABOUT ALL THIS, CORNELIA.
I HOPE HANNAH WILL FORGIVE ME SOMEDAY.
SHE'S **UPSET**, DREW.
YOU CAN'T **POSSIBLY** IMAGINE WHAT IT'S LIKE TO BE A **MOTHER**.
THERE'S **NOTHING** SHE WON'T DO TO FIND HER SON.
YEAH. MOMS CAN BE **INTENSE**.
HA! INDEED.
MY MOTHER, SHE WASN'T AN EASY WOMAN TO DEAL WITH.
BUT SHE WAS... **FORMIDABLE**.
I GUESS I MIGHT HAVE INHERITED A **LITTLE** OF THAT.
OR... **A LOT** OF THAT?

THE PAINTINGS IN THIS WING WERE HER PASSION, HER **LIFE'S WORK**.
SHE DONATED THEM TO THE INSTITUTE SO THAT THEY WOULD BE TAKEN CARE OF...
SO THEY WOULD LIVE ON LONG AFTER **SHE** DID.
I HOPE THEY **WILL**, CORNELIA.
I HOPE I CAN HELP.
DID YOU **GROW UP** WITH THESE PAINTINGS, GRAMMY?
ARE THEY **THAT** OLD?!
HA HA, THEY'RE EVEN OLDER THAN **ME**! CAN YOU **IMAGINE**?
WHOA.

OOH, WHEN I WAS YOUR AGE...
THIS WAS MY FAVORITE.
WHY THIS ONE?
IT'S JUST TREES AND COWS.
I AGREE, THAD.
NOT VERY EXCITING.
WELL, THAT'S THE POINT, MY DEARS...

IT'S ALWAYS BEEN MY TINY LITTLE PAINTED **PARADISE**.
BLISSFULLY QUIET AND PEACEFUL.
AN...**ESCAPE**.

TAKE IT ALL IN, CHILDREN.
LET THE RIVER FLOW BY, FEEL THE WIND ON YOUR FACE.
HEAR THE GENTLE MOO OF A COW.
NO MATTER WHAT TROUBLES YOU FACE IN THE REAL WORLD...

NONE OF THAT CAN FIND YOU HERE.

RR?

LICK
LICK

LEVI!
WE WERE HAVING A **MOMENT**!
EE?

I'M SORRY, CORNELIA.
LEVI IS... UNPREDICTABLE.
YES, I'VE GATHERED THAT.

HE'S KIND OF...

EVERYTHING GOOD AND BAD IN ME...
ALL MIXED TOGETHER.

HOW DID HE DO THAT?
JUST NOW?
WHERE DID HE GO?

I DUNNO, HE MUST HAVE TRAVELED TO AN L STOP.
I DREW SOME FOR MY FRIENDS AND FOR RICKY'S DOODLE DINER.

AND HE CAN ALWAYS TRAVEL BACK TO ME, OF COURSE.
BECAUSE WE'RE SO CONNECTED, I GUESS.
WOWWW!

BUT...
I DON'T FOLLOW.
HOW CAN YOU NOT UNDERSTAND YOUR OWN DRAWING?
HOW CAN SOMETHING YOU MADE SURPRISE YOU?
HA HA, CORNELIA!
DON'T BE OFFENDED, BUT...
FOR SOMEONE WHO'S SO OBSESSED WITH ART...
YOU DON'T SEEM TO UNDERSTAND A LOT ABOUT CREATIVITY.

MOOOOOO!

HA HA HA!

ZEN! DID YOU SEE--?

I'M KINDA **BUSY**, AMEER!

DID YOU FIND SOMETHING?
YEAH, THERE ARE PEOPLE STUCK IN THIS WRECKED DINER.
CAN YOU HELP ME GET THEM OUT?

BUT WE NEED TO FOLLOW THAT CLOWN!
SEE WHERE--
AMEER!!

OKAY, FINE, BUT WE HAVE TO BE QUICK!
WOW, HOW HEROIC.

THANKS, AMEER.
I'M SO GLAD YOU COULD FIND TIME TO SAVE SOME INNOCENT CIVILIANS IN YOUR BUSY SUPERHERO SCHEDULE.
THAT'S NOT FAIR, ZEN!
WE'RE SUPPOSED TO BE FOLLOWING THE BAD GUYS!
FINDING THE BABY!
BUT WE HAVE TO HELP ANYONE WE CAN, AMEER.
HOW CAN YOU JUST PASS THEM BY?

THESE PEOPLE DIDN'T PICK A **SIDE**.
THEY DIDN'T **WANT** TO BE A PART OF THIS.
BUT THEIR HOMES WERE **RUINED** ANYWAY.
NOW THERE'S NOWHERE **SAFE** FOR THEM TO GO.
NOT UNTIL THE FIGHTING STOPS.
SO WE HAVE TO...
AMEER?!

SHOW US WHERE YOU'VE GOT THE BABY, OR...
OR **ELSE**!
SERIOUSLY, AMEER?
YOU THINK **HE'S** THREATENED BY CAPTAIN COCKATOO?
WHAT DO YOU MEAN?
YOU DON'T THINK CAP COULD TAKE HIM IN A FIGHT?
THAT'S NOT THE **POINT**!!
FIGHTING JUST MAKES EVERYTHING **WORSE**!
WE SHOULD BE **TALKING** TO PEOPLE! **HELPING** THEM!
THAT'S WHAT A **REAL** HERO DOES!
BUT...
IN **REAL LIFE,** AMEER.
NOT SOME STUPID COMIC BOOK!

HE...
HE'S GETTING AWAY!
CAP! GET HIM!

PAF!

GRAB

RIIIIIIP

DON'T!!

PLEASE DON'T HURT HIM!

LET HIM **GO**!

I DON'T KNOW WHAT I'D DO IF...

IF...

CRASH!!

CAP!

I TOLD YOU, AMEER!
ZEN...
THAT DIDN'T HAVE TO HAPPEN!
SO...WHAT, ZEN? WOULD YOU RATHER HAVE THE MAGICAL BUTTERFLY BOYFRIENDS JUST HOLD HANDS AND FIX EVERYTHING WITH THEIR LOVE MAGIC?!
YEAH! MAYBE!
I WAS JUST... I WAS JOKING, ZEN.
WELL, I WASN'T.
NOW COME ON.
I HAVE AN IDEA.

IN THE MODERN ART WING...
MY SCANS AREN'T PICKING UP ANY SIGNS OF THE BABY. HMM...
IT'S LIKE HE JUST... VANISHED!
ARE YOU HAVING ANY LUCK IN THERE, TJ?

WHA--?! WHAT ARE YOU DOING?!
THAT'S ONE OF DORIAN'S DARK ART SOLDIERS!
YEAH, HE'S TEACHING ME A SPELL.
BUT... HE'S EVIL!
OR AT LEAST STRANGE.
CREEPY.
OF HIGHLY QUESTIONABLE CHARACTER.
I KNOW, HE'S AWESOME.
THAT'S NOT WHAT I--
WAIT. WHAT KIND OF SPELL IS IT?
HERE, I'LL SHOW YOU.
ON GLOOP?
YEAH, HE VOLUNTEERED!

EEEEE!
BLOOOO!
KSSHHH!
AA?
TJ!
WHAT DID YOU DO TO **GLOOP**?!
I'M NOT SURE, BUT IT'S THE COOLEST THING I'VE EVER DONE!
"COOL"??
TURN HIM BACK TO **NORMAL**!
CAN YOU TURN HIM BACK?
YEAH. PROBABLY?

YOU KNOW HOW IT IS.
MAGIC IS **WEIRD**.

YEAH!
WHICH IS EXACTLY MY **PROBLEM** WITH IT!

YOU HAVE A **PROBLEM** WITH MY...?
IT'S **WEIRD** AND **MESSY** AND **MAKES NO SENSE**!

WELL, BECK.
THE **WHOLE WORLD** IS WEIRD.
IT'S MESSY, AND IT DOESN'T ALWAYS **MAKE SENSE**.

YOU MIGHT LIKE ANSWERS AND EXPLANATIONS.
BUT SOME THINGS CAN'T BE EXPLAINED.
SOME THINGS ARE WEIRD. AND WONDERFUL.
THEY'RE STRANGE AND CREEPY AND MORE INCREDIBLE THAN YOU COULD EVER IMAGINE.

I...
I NEED TO GET OUT OF HERE.
SO SOON?
MAYBE DINAH WOULD LIKE...
A MAGICAL MAKEOVER?
DON'T YOU DARE!!
WHAT?!
GEEZ.

BECK!
C'MON!
BZZT
I...
HUH?!
A **FORCE FIELD**?
SERIOUSLY?!
I WAS JUST **TEASING**, BECK.
I WOULDN'T ACTUALLY...
YOU DON'T THINK I UNDERSTAND **TEASING**?
LIKE I DON'T GET TEASED **ENOUGH** ALREADY?
YOU?!
ABOUT **WHAT**?
ABOUT HOW I **LOOK**.
AND ABOUT HOW I **THINK**.

SOME PEOPLE THINK I'M **SLOW**.
AND SOME THINK I'M A **SUPER-GENIUS**.

BUT I'M NOT EITHER OF THOSE.
IT'S JUST HOW MY BRAIN WORKS.
AND I CAN'T TURN THAT OFF, EVEN IF I **WANT** TO.

...EVEN IF I GET **TEASED** ABOUT IT.

I KNOW, BECK.
I WASN'T TRYING TO **MAKE FUN** OF YOU.

IT'S TOO MUCH, TJ.
YOUR... MESSY WAY OF SEEING THE WORLD.
I CAN'T LIVE LIKE THAT.
I NEED ANSWERS AND EXPLANATIONS TO UNDERSTAND WHAT I'M LOOKING AT...
I NEED PLANS. I NEED... PREPARATION.
BUT YOU CAN ANALYZE SOMETHING FOREVER, BECK.
AT SOME POINT YOU'VE GOTTA DO SOMETHING.
BUT YOU'VE GOT TO DO IT RIGHT.
EVEN IF THAT TAKES TIME.

I LIKE TO LOOK **CLOSELY**, TAKE THINGS **SLOWLY**.
SEE THE UNDERLYING ORDER IN **EVERYTHING**.
CATEGORIZE, **ORGANIZE**.

I CAN BREAK DOWN **ANY PROBLEM** INTO SIMPLE LITTLE PIECES.
AND ONCE I DO THAT, I CAN PUT EVERYTHING **BACK TOGETHER**.
LIKE A BIG, BEAUTIFUL **PUZZLE**.

OKAY, I GET IT.
I'VE BEEN A **BUTT**.

NOW...CAN YOU DROP THIS **FORCE FIELD**?

FINE.
BUT I'VE HAD **ENOUGH** OF YOUR **MAGIC** FOR TODAY.

ELSEWHERE IN THE INSTITUTE...
WAIT, YOU WANT TO DO **WHAT**?!

IT'S LIKE I SAID BEFORE.
NOT THAT YOU WERE ACTUALLY **LISTENING**...

UNTIL THE **FIGHTING** STOPS, THERE ISN'T A SAFE PLACE TO GO IN THE INSTITUTE.

SO... I'M GOING TO **MAKE** ONE.
BUT... **HERE**?!

ISN'T IT PERFECT?
NOW I JUST NEED TO DRAW SOME BUILDING SUPPLIES...
BUT...
BOOM

WHAT WAS THAT?!
I DON'T KNOW, BUT--
AMEER!!

OH, DANG.
IT'S THEM!!
BOOM BOOM
THE DARK ART ARMY!
THE CLOWN, HE'S GOT A DRUM!
LIKE THEY'RE MARCHING OFF TO WAR!
AND--
WHOA!
IT'S HANNAH AND HER WARRIORS!
OH MAN!

AMEER! DO YOU KNOW WHAT'S GOING ON?
IT'S GOTTA BE THE **FINAL SHOWDOWN**!
WAIT, WHAT HAPPENED TO CAPTAIN COCKATOO?
OH.
UH...
IT WAS THE CLOWN. HE--
CAP IS FINE.
HE'S **FINE**.
WHY IS HE **PINK**?
WHAT DO YOU **MEAN** "WHY IS HE PINK?"
HA HA, HE'S SILLY.
HE IS **NOT** SILLY!!

WAIT, THEY'RE NOT FIGHTING!

THEY'RE... TALKING?
MAYBE THEY'LL CALL A TRUCE?
IS THAT A THING?

SHOW THEM, CAPTAIN COCKATOO!
HUH?

WAIT! AMEER!!
DON'T--
BOOM

AMEER, WHAT DID YOU DO?!
WE HAVE TO TAKE A STAND!
WE--
WE CAN BEAT THEM!
WE CAN END THIS!
AT WHAT COST?
THIS IS A CATASTROPHE.
DORIAN, STOP!!
YOU'RE BETTER THAN THIS!

REMEMBER ME?
I DREW YOU THAT BANDAGE WHEN YOU GOT BITTEN.
I KNOW YOU DIDN'T TAKE THE BABY.
I DON'T THINK YOU'RE A MONSTER.
I THINK THIS HAS ALL BEEN A HUGE MISUNDERSTANDING.
AND TOGETHER WE CAN--
HUH?!

WHAT-- WHAT'S HAPPENING?!
THE SICK NEW SPELL I LEARNED.
YOU'RE WELCOME.
TJ, YOU HAVE TO STOP!
WHY? IT'S WORKING!

TJ, I TOLD YOU!
YOU DON'T KNOW WHAT THE MAGIC IS DOING!
I THINK IT'S PRETTY CLEAR WHAT IT'S DOING.
HE'S IN PAIN!
YOU'RE HURTING HIM!
DINAH, YOU'VE GOT TO STOP BRU!
QUICK!
HURRY!!
DON'T YOU DARE, DINAH!

BUTTERFLY BOYFRIENDS, HELP DINAH!
STOP THE SPELL!!
NO, CAP! HELP BRU! TJ IS RIGHT!
DREW, CAN'T YOU GET LEVI TO HELP?!
WE NEED HIM!
BUT--
I DON'T WANT TO PICK A SIDE!
WE'RE HERE FOR THE BABY, NOT TO FIGHT!
WE'VE GOT TO STOP THIS BEFORE--

BAM!!
CAP!
DINAH!
MY PRINCES!
HE'S OKAY.
CAPTAIN COCKATOO IS OKAY.
BUT... **DORIAN**... HE...

AAAR

HE IS DEFINITELY NOT OKAY.

CHAPTER 4:
DEFINITELY
NOT OKAY

LATER THAT DAY...
DING-DONG!

HMM?
WHO COULD **THAT** BE?

DREW?
MR. SCHNEIDER?
YOU TOLD US TO, UH, STAY OUT OF **TROUBLE,** BUT...
UH-OH.
TELL ME EVERYTHING.

HE-- HE WAS **SCREAMING**.

LIKE HE WAS ANGRY. OR...**IN PAIN**.

I DON'T THINK HE UNDERSTOOD WHAT HAD HAPPENED.

I DON'T, EITHER.

HE STARTED LASHING OUT AT **EVERYONE** AROUND HIM.

I WANTED TO STAY AND HELP, BUT CORNELIA DRAGGED US AWAY.

CORNELIA MUST HAVE BEEN **FURIOUS**.
I-- SHE--
SHE WAS **WORRIED**.

I CAN'T LET YOU GET CAUGHT UP IN THIS **CARNAGE**.
I'M TAKING YOU **HOME**.

AND SO... DORIAN IS **RUNNING LOOSE**?
RAMPAGING THROUGH THE INSTITUTE?
THAT'S NOT EVEN THE **WORST** PART.

WHAT?!
THERE'S **MORE**?

THE VERY WORST PART WAS...
THE RIDE HOME.
SHE THINKS SHE'S ALWAYS RIGHT, BUT SOMETIMES IT'S NOT SO SIMPLE--
YOU DIDN'T EVEN KNOW WHAT THAT SPELL WOULD DO!
NEEDLESS AGGRESSION AND YOUR BIG EGO
WOULDN'T EVEN PICK A SIDE AND HELP US WHEN YOU GOT IN THE MIDDLE THE
RECKLESS USE OF MAGIC THAT RESULTED IN--
HE HAD NO PLAN, AND NOW WE'RE ALL STUCK CLEANING UP HIS MESS!
YEAH? WELL, WHAT WOULD YOU HAVE DONE THEN, HUH?!
THEIR FAULT THAT IT EVEN GOT TO THAT POINT AND
ZENOBIA WOULD RATHER LET THOSE MONSTERS RUN FREE INSTEAD OF--
IT NEVER WOULD HAVE HAPPENED IF AMEER WASN'T ITCHING FOR A FIGHT AND--
IF YOU HAD JUST LISTENED TO ME--
OH, COME ON!
ARE YOU SERIOUS?

WE'VE NEVER **FOUGHT** LIKE THAT!
EVERYONE WAS **SO ANGRY**, AND THEY SAID **AWFUL** THINGS TO EACH OTHER!
IT WAS AN **INCREDIBLY STRESSFUL** SITUATION, DREW.
ANYONE WOULD HAVE BEEN UPSET.

BUT IT'S **MORE** THAN THAT, MR. SCHNEIDER.
JOINING ART CLUB HAS BEEN THE **BEST THING** THAT'S EVER HAPPENED TO ME.
THEY'RE MY ONLY FRIENDS.

AND NOW THEY **HATE** EACH OTHER.
BECAUSE OF **ME** AND THE MESS I MADE.
DREW...

I THINK I **RUINED** ART CLUB.

THAT'S NOT TRUE **AT ALL,** DREW.
I'M SURE WE CAN WORK THIS OUT.
HOW?

I MAY NOT BE IN SCHOOL FOR A WHILE, BUT...
I'M STILL YOUR **TEACHER**.
I'M HERE TO HELP YOU THROUGH ALL OF THIS.

AND I'LL GET US SOME MORE COOKIES.

THANKS, MR. SCHNEIDER.
FOR... **EVERYTHING**.

HI, EVERYONE...
I WANTED TO SAY I'M SORRY.
I'M SO SO SO SO SORRY FOR EVERYTHING THAT HAPPENED TODAY.
BZZT
BZZT
BZZT

WE WERE ALL JUST TRYING TO HELP MR. SCHNEIDER AND THE INSTITUTE...
EVEN IF WE HAD DIFFERENT IDEAS ABOUT HOW TO DO THAT.
DING
DING

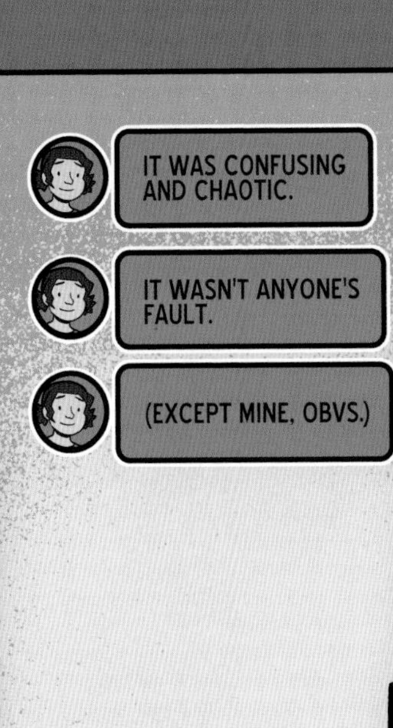
IT WAS CONFUSING AND CHAOTIC.
IT WASN'T ANYONE'S FAULT.
(EXCEPT MINE, OBVS.)

I JUST WANT US TO BE OKAY.
ARE WE GOING TO BE OKAY?
BZZT BZZT

...IS ANYONE THERE????

LOOK WHAT I PICKED UP AT THE COMIC SHOP, ZEN!
THE NEW PRETTY PRINCE ACADEMY!
I GRABBED THE LAST COPY.
FOUGHT A LITTLE GIRL FOR IT.
AND I'LL EVEN LET YOU READ IT FIRST!
THAT'S OKAY, GRANDMA.
YOU CAN READ IT IF YOU WANT.
YOU-- YOU'D RATHER READ WHATEVER THAT IS?!
DON'T YOU WANT TO SEE WHO GETS CROWNED THE PRETTIEST PRINCE?
YEAH, BUT LATER.
HUH.
THE PICTURE OF DORIAN GRAY.
IS THAT FOR SCHOOL?
NO.
IS IT GOOD?
NO, IT'S AWFUL.

ZENOBIA, HONEY, **WHY** ARE YOU READING AN AWFUL BOOK?!

BECAUSE I HAVE TO!

I **NEED** TO KNOW HIS **STORY**!!

WHOSE?

DORIAN GRAY'S?

BUT...

I GUESS I'LL LET YOU FINISH, THEN.

THANKS.

MIND IF I DIG INTO PRETTY PRINCE ACADEMY?

SURE. BUT NO SPOILERS.

GIRL, OF **COURSE** NOT.

AT THE DINER...
NO ONE'S TEXTING BACK.
THEY MUST **HATE** ME.
NO ONE **HATES** YOU, DREW.
HOW COULD THEY **HATE** YOU?
EVERYONE HANDLES THIS KIND OF THING IN THEIR OWN WAY.
TJ LISTENS TO A SAD PLAYLIST AND TELLS ME TO GO AWAY.
YOU'RE NOT HUNGRY?
YOU BARELY ATE.
YEAH. NO.

ARE THE DOODLES HUNGRY?
TONIGHT'S SPECIAL IS **SPIDER SUSHI**.

SPIDER SUSHI?
THAT SOUNDS **GROSS**.

AND TOTALLY **AWESOME**.
CAN I SEE?
SURE!

DREW.
CAN WE TALK?
CORNELIA?
EWWW!
HA HA!

SO...
HOW BAD
IS IT?
IT'S...BAD.
IF THERE'S ANYTHING I CAN DO...
I'M GOING BACK TONIGHT TO ASSESS THE SITUATION.
I APPRECIATE IT, DREW.
I APPRECIATE ALL YOU'VE **TRIED** TO DO.
AND I'LL HAVE THE CHARGES AGAINST MR. SCHNEIDER DROPPED.
BUT...
I CAN'T INVOLVE YOU CHILDREN IN THIS ANY LONGER.
I GUESS I UNDERSTAND.

THAD?
IT'S TIME TO GO.
BUT-- BUT RICKY MADE SPIDER SUSHI!
AND I'M DRAWING COBWEB CURRY TO GO WITH IT!
THAT SOUNDS... **LOVELY**...BUT I'VE GOT A **LONG NIGHT** AHEAD OF ME.
UM, CORNELIA...?

LATER THAT NIGHT...
DREW?
YOU'RE STILL UP?
ARE YOU WORKING ON DOODLEVILLE STUFF?
DOODLEVILLE IS GONE, MOM.
REMEMBER?
RIGHT, BUT...
WEREN'T YOU GOING TO DRAW...
A **NEW** DOODLEVILLE?
YEAH.
I WANTED TO.
BUT...
WHAT IF IT'S NOT AS GOOD AS BEFORE?
WHAT IF IT'S **RUINED** AGAIN?
WHAT IF IT'S JUST **ANOTHER** THING THAT I MESS UP?
YOU'RE WRESTLING WITH **A LOT** RIGHT NOW.
DON'T BE SO HARD ON YOURSELF, DREW.
I'M JUST SO SICK OF **DISAPPOINTING** PEOPLE.

OH, MY SWEET GIRL.
YOU'VE BEEN THROUGH **SO MUCH.**
YOU'VE **DONE** SO MUCH.
BUT YOU'VE **NEVER** DISAPPOINTED ME.
I JUST...
I WISH I COULD FIGURE OUT HOW TO **FIX** THINGS.
ART CLUB, DORIAN GRAY, EVERYTHING ELSE AT THE INSTITUTE.
I WISH EVERYTHING COULD BE LIKE IT **USED** TO BE.
LIKE IT USED TO BE?
WHEN DRAWING WAS SO **EASY** FOR ME.
...WHEN IT WAS **FUN**.

AT THE INSTITUTE...
MRS. KRONG?

MRS. KRONG!
YOU SHOULD COME AND SEE THIS!

SORRY, I... WHAT IS IT?
MORE... FIGHTING?
I'VE SEEN **FAR** TOO MUCH OF THAT ALREADY.
NO, IT'S NOT THAT AT ALL.

THIS?
WHAT IS THIS?
WHERE ARE THEY GOING?
THEY'RE TAKING REFUGE IN THE CLOUD FORTRESS.
THE... WHAT?
THERE'S NO "CLOUD FORTRESS" IN THIS INSTITUTE.
I WOULD KNOW!
I MEAN, REALLY.
NO, JUST LOOK. IN THERE.

WHAT? WHO? **HOW?**

WE THINK IT WAS ONE OF THE CHILDREN.

THOSE BUTTERFLY BOYS SEEM TO BE IN CHARGE.

THEY'VE BEEN GIVING SHELTER TO ANYONE WHO NEEDS IT.

LEVI!
WHAT'S GOING ON HERE?
YOU... KNOW HIM?
WE'VE... MET.
WAIT.
THAT'S AN L STOP.
DREW SAID LEVI USES THOSE TO--
WHAT?! HE--
WHERE DID HE GO?!
THAT'S... A GOOD QUESTION.

HUH?
LEVI? IS THAT YOU?
WHAT'S--?
WHAT?!
WHO--?
THEY--
YOU **CAN'T** KEEP TAKING PEOPLE FROM THE INSTITUTE, LEVI!!
CORNELIA'S GONNA BE **FURIOUS**!
AND--
AND--

IT--
IT MUST BE PRETTY BAD THERE, HUH?
IT'S NOT SAFE AT THE INSTITUTE ANYMORE, IS IT?
I'M SO SORRY.
WHAT CAN I **DO** FOR ALL OF YOU?
ARE YOU HUNGRY? TIRED?
WHAT DO YOU NEED?
WAIT, LEVI, WHERE ARE YOU GOING?
ARE THERE **MORE**?
WE'RE GONNA NEED MORE ROOM AND--
LEVI!
DOES **CORNELIA** KNOW ABOUT THIS?!

CHAPTER 5: THE ART INSTITUTE EXODUS

L

LEVI, WHAT THE HECK?!
ARE THEY FROM THE INSTITUTE?!
WHAT ARE THEY DOING **HERE**?

HEY, EVERYONE. UM... DID LEVI VISIT EACH OF YOU THIS MORNING?

I...I THINK IT'S MY FAULT.

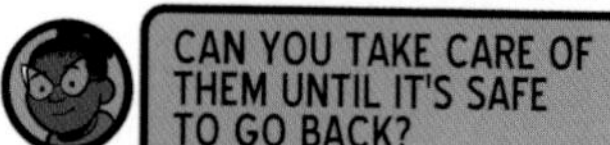
CAN YOU TAKE CARE OF THEM UNTIL IT'S SAFE TO GO BACK?

BZZT
BZZT

UGH!!
SERIOUSLY?!
HEY, KIDDO, WHAT'S WRONG?

ZENOBIA IS WHAT'S WRONG!
SHE'D RATHER EMPTY OUT THE ART INSTITUTE THAN DEAL WITH THE REAL PROBLEM!
EMPTY OUT...?
HUH?

SHE SAYS FIGHTING JUST MAKES EVERYTHING WORSE.
WELL, HOW ELSE ARE WE GONNA STOP DORIAN?
CAPTAIN COCKATOO HAD TO DO SOMETHING.

HOLD UP-- WHO WAS CAP FIGHTING?
HIS NAME IS DORIAN GRAY.
BIG GIANT SCARY PAINTING DUDE.

BUT WAIT...
HELLO!
HELLO!
WHAT WAS THIS DORIAN GUY DOING?
THREATENING SOMEBODY?
HURTING THEM?
HE--HE WAS TALKING.
WITH THIS LADY HANNAH AND--
TALKING?
AND HE TOOK THE BABY!
PROBABLY!
SQUAWK!
HE WAS DEFINITELY UP TO SOMETHING!
SO YOU STARTED THE FIGHT?
YOU AND CAPTAIN COCKATOO?
WHAT? NO.
I...
I MEAN... MAYBE.

WHAT HAPPENED THEN? ONCE THE FIGHT STARTED?
IT-- **A LOT** HAPPENED. IT WAS CONFUSING.

THINGS GOT OUT OF CONTROL, AND...
IT WAS **BAD**.
REALLY BAD.
SO...
IT SOUNDS LIKE FIGHTING **DID** MAKE EVERYTHING WORSE.

ARE YOU SAYING THAT I MESSED UP?
MAYBE.
WHAT MATTERS NOW IS WHAT YOU **DO** ABOUT IT.
BUT, HEY, NOBODY'S PERFECT.
NOT ME, NOT EVEN CAPTAIN COCKATOO.

YOU KNOW, I'VE NEVER SEEN CAP WITHOUT HIS MASK!
HE SORT OF LOOKS LIKE...
IS HE BASED ON **ME**?!
DAD.

MAYBE YOU'RE RIGHT ABOUT CAP.
HE'S **NOT** PERFECT.
AT LEAST, NOT **YET**.
CAPTAIN COCKATOO NEEDS TO MAJORLY **LEVEL UP** IF HE'S GONNA TAKE ON DORIAN.
UH, THAT'S NOT REALLY WHAT I WAS SAYING...
HE NEEDS TO BE STRONGER, MORE SERIOUS.
I'LL DESIGN A WHOLE NEW COSTUME, LIKE WITH ARMOR AND WEAPONS...
I'LL START SKETCHING AFTER BREAKFAST.
THERE ARE LOTS OF DIFFERENT WAYS TO BE **STRONG**, AMEER.
AND LOTS OF WAYS TO BE A **HERO**.

WELL, RIGHT NOW, EVERYONE THINKS HE'S JUST SILLY.
AND PINK.
HEY! WHAT'S WRONG WITH PINK?
WHAT'S WRONG WITH SILLY?!
YOUR MOM SAYS I'M SILLY.
SOMETHING WRONG WITH THAT?
I'M BEING SERIOUS, DAD.
ME TOO. THIS IS SERIOUS.
SO TELL ME THE TRUTH...
WHO'S GOT BIGGER BICEPS, ME OR CAPTAIN COCKATOO?
HA HA!
ME, RIGHT?

AT THE DINER...

UH, DREW?
THAT WAS... MRS. KRONG.

SHE WANTS TO SEE YOU.
AND ZENOBIA.
AT...THE INSTITUTE.

UGH, SHE MUST **NOT** BE HAPPY ABOUT LEVI'S LITTLE TRIPS.
WHY NOT? HE BRINGS THE **BEST** SURPRISES!

THE DOODLE DINER **IS** PRETTY BUSY. CAN YOU KEEP UP?
I'VE HAD **A LOT** OF PRACTICE LATELY.
I'LL MANAGE.

LATER THAT DAY...
THANKS FOR BRINGING US, MR. SCHNEIDER.

OF COURSE!
I COULDN'T LET YOU FACE CORNELIA **ALONE**, COULD I?
HOPEFULLY--

THE ART INSTITUTE IS **CLOSED**.

UM... WE SORT OF HAVE AN APPOINTMENT WITH--

THEY'RE WITH **ME**.
OH!

SORRY, MRS. KRONG.
RIGHT THIS WAY.

MRS. KRONG, WE WERE JUST TRYING TO **HELP**.
YEAH, WE WEREN'T, UH, **STEALING** ALL THOSE PAINTINGS, JUST GIVING THEM A SAFE PLACE TO STAY.
FOR NOW.

I DREW THE FORTRESS AS A REFUGE...
BUT IT'S JUST NOT BIG ENOUGH FOR EVERYONE.
RIGHT, AND SO...

THIS IS **YOUR** WORK, YOUNG LADY?
YES, MA'AM.

BUT IT'S NOT ZEN'S FAULT!
IT'S LEVI-- I DIDN'T ASK HIM TO, BUT HE'S BEEN DOING AS MANY TRIPS AS HE CAN, AND--
HE JUST WANTS THEM TO BE SAFE, SO--
I KNOW WHAT HE'S DONE.
I'VE WATCHED HIM COME AND GO A DOZEN TIMES WITH AS MANY PEOPLE AS HE CAN CARRY.
I'M SO SORRY-- I TOLD YOU HE HAS A MIND OF HIS OWN.
THIS HAS ALL BEEN A HUGE MISTAKE.
NO, MY DEAR. THIS IS NO MISTAKE.
THIS...
IS EXTRAORDINARY.

YOU--
YOU'RE NOT **MAD**?
I'M **FURIOUS**, ACTUALLY.
BUT **NOT** AT YOU CHILDREN.
NOR AT **YOU**, MR. SCHNEIDER.
THE ONLY ONE WORTHY OF MY ANGER IS THE **MONSTER** RAMPAGING THROUGH THIS INSTITUTE.
DORIAN?
WHERE IS HE?
IS HE **OKAY**?
I'M SORRY...
ARE YOU ASKING WHETHER THE CREATURE CURRENTLY **DESTROYING** EVERY ARTWORK IN THIS INSTITUTE IS... **OKAY**?
UM... YES?

A FEW MINUTES LATER...
DORIAN? HI.
IT'S ME AGAIN.
I WANTED TO SAY... I'M SORRY.
FOR EVERYTHING THAT'S BEEN DONE TO YOU.
FOR EVERYONE TREATING YOU LIKE A MONSTER.
YOU'RE SORRY?
THAT HE'S A MONSTER?
BUT... HE'S NOT.
HAVEN'T YOU READ HIS BOOK?
HIS BOOK?
THE PICTURE OF DORIAN GRAY.
OH DEAR.
YEAH, IT'S SUPER GROSS AND CREEPY.
NOT REALLY APPROPRIATE FOR KIDS. OOPS.

BUT WHAT'S THE BOOK **ABOUT**?

IT'S ABOUT A YOUNG MAN NAMED DORIAN AND A PORTRAIT THAT'S PAINTED OF HIM.
THEY'RE CONNECTED.

WHATEVER BAD THINGS HAPPEN TO **DORIAN** MAGICALLY SHOW UP ON THE **PAINTING** INSTEAD.
IT'S HIS **PAINTING** THAT GETS OLD, SICK, AND SCARRED.
BUT DORIAN STAYS YOUNG AND BEAUTIFUL, NO MATTER WHAT.

AND SO DORIAN DOES WHATEVER HE WANTS.
BUT EVEN THOUGH HE STILL **LOOKS** THE SAME...
HE BECOMES A **MONSTER**.

YOU THINK **THAT'S** THE CURSED PAINTING?
WHATEVER HE IS, HE KEEPS SUFFERING FOR EVERYONE ELSE'S MISTAKES.
IT'S JUST A BOOK, THOUGH.
RIGHT?!

WE'VE TREATED HIM LIKE A MONSTER THIS WHOLE TIME INSTEAD OF TRYING TO SEE **HIS SIDE** OF THE STORY.
IT'S NOT FAIR TO HIM, AND IT'S MADE EVERYTHING **WORSE**.

I-- I THINK YOU'RE **RIGHT**.
I DON'T KNOW HOW TO MAKE UP FOR EVERYTHING THAT'S BEEN DONE TO HIM, BUT...
I **MIGHT** KNOW WHERE TO **START**.

THIS ALL BEGAN WITH THE MISSING BABY, RIGHT?
AND... THE **CAT**.
THE **STATUE** OF THE CAT.

I GUESS IT'S REALLY A **PAINTING** OF A STATUE OF A CAT.
WHICH...IS WEIRD.
WHERE ARE YOU GOING WITH ALL THIS, DREW?

WHEN JUNIOR WENT MISSING AGAIN, HANNAH **COULD HAVE** ASKED DORIAN TO HELP **FIND** HIM.
BUT SHE TREATED HIM LIKE A MONSTER AND **SHATTERED** PRETTY MUCH THE ONLY FRIEND HE EVER REALLY HAD.
HIS **CAT**.

SO YOU WANT TO FIX IT?
THE CAT?
BUT ITS PIECES ARE SCATTERED ALL OVER THE INSTITUTE!
RIGHT.
IT'S NOT GOING TO BE EASY, BUT...
I THINK MY DOODLES CAN FIND THEM.
IT COULD BE POSSIBLE.
BUT IT WILL CERTAINLY BE DANGEROUS.
I KNOW.
GRRRR

DORIAN'S STILL **ANGRY**, AND--
HE'S **NOT** THINKING CLEARLY LIKE THIS.
TJ NEEDS TO FIGURE OUT HOW TO REVERSE THE SPELL.
AND **FAST**.
WHAT ABOUT THE **BABY**?
UNTIL WE FIND **JUNIOR**, HANNAH WON'T BACK DOWN.
DO YOU KNOW WHERE HE IS?
NO, NOT YET.
BUT... I THINK **LEVI** DOES.
BECAUSE... **YOU'RE** THE ONE THAT TOOK HIM, AREN'T YOU?

THAT EVENING, IN THE SHARED BEDROOM OF TJ AND RICKY...
HEY, TJ, LOOK AT WHAT I DREW!

I'M **BUSY**, RICKY.
I'M TRYING TO FIX GLOOP.
WHY?

BECAUSE I MESSED UP.
I CAN'T GET HIM BACK TO **NORMAL**.
WHY?

I DON'T **KNOW**!
THIS STUFF IS COMPLICATED AND I CAN'T UNDERSTAND IT.
BUT...
WHY?

I DON'T **KNOW**!!
MAYBE BECK WAS **RIGHT**.
UGH, IT **HURTS** EVEN **SAYING** THAT.
I BET IT DOES.
YOU'RE **SUPER** STUBBORN.

NOW, WHAT DID YOU WANT TO--
RICKY!!
WHAT?
OH, RIGHT.
I DREW SOME NEW OUTFITS FOR OUR ART INSTITUTE VISITORS.
BUT... WHY?
WHAT DID YOU DO WITH THEIR CLOTHES?
THEY DIDN'T HAVE ANY.
THEY WERE NAKED?!
YUP.

KIDS?
YOU HAVE A GUEST!
HI.
DREW!!
WHAT'S UP?

UM...
I'M HERE FOR THE BABY.

WHAT, YOU THINK I HAD SOMETHING TO DO WITH HIM GOING MISSING?
EVERYONE BLAMES ME FOR EVERYTHING!!

UHHHH...
I THINK SHE WAS TALKING TO ME.

WHAT DO YOU--?
RICKY!!!

LEVI SHOWED UP ONE NIGHT WITH HIM, AND...
HE'S BEEN **HERE** THE WHOLE TIME?!
I TRIED TO KEEP HIM SAFE AND HIDDEN.
AND **FED,** OF COURSE!
I'M SORRY IF IT WAS **BAD** TO KEEP HIM SECRET.
BUT-- BUT EVERYTHING THAT'S HAPPENED AT THE INSTITUTE...
HE WAS JUST TRYING TO **HELP,** TJ.
AND SO WAS LEVI.
WE'LL GET HIM BACK TO HIS MOM. AS SOON AS IT'S SAFE AT THE INSTITUTE.
THAT...
MIGHT BE A WHILE.

LATER THAT NIGHT, AT THE INSTITUTE...
SLAM!

EEE!!

THE NEXT MORNING...
MORNING, KIDDO!
READY FOR SCHOOL?

ALMOST. I'M JUST...
THERE, DONE.
OH? DID YOU DRAW A NEW COSTUME FOR CAPTAIN COCKATOO?

NOT EXACTLY. I JUST FIXED UP THE OLD ONE.

HE'S SHOWING OFF THAT HANDSOME FACE!
WHAT ABOUT HIS **SECRET IDENTITY**?

WHY KEEP IT **SECRET**? IF HE HAPPENS TO LOOK A **LITTLE** LIKE MY DAD...
THAT'S **NOT** SOMETHING I NEED TO HIDE.
AWW!!

YOU KEPT HIS CLASSIC PINK COSTUME, THOUGH.
IT'S NOT TOO SILLY?
NAH.
GOOD! SOME OF MY FAVORITE SUPERHEROES ARE SILLY.
THAT'S WHAT I LIKE ABOUT THEM.
BEING A HERO IS MORE THAN JUST BEATING UP BAD GUYS.
YEAH, IT'S INSPIRING PEOPLE TO BE THEIR BEST, RIGHT?
AND HELPING THEM AT THEIR WORST.
AND MAYBE BEING A LITTLE SILLY?
RIGHT ON, CAP!
WE'RE BIRDS OF A FEATHER.
BUMP
NOOO!! IT'S TOO EARLY FOR DAD JOKES!
STOP SQUAWKING AND GET READY FOR SCHOOL, YOUNG MAN!
DAAAAAD!!!
WHAT DO YOU WANT FOR BREAKFAST? EGGS?

LATER, AT SCHOOL...

SO THE BABY'S OKAY?
YEAH, RICKY TOOK GOOD CARE OF HIM.
AND LEVI VISITED EVERY NIGHT.
LEVI'S BEEN **BUSY**!
HE'S RESCUED SO MANY PEOPLE FROM THE INSTITUTE!
YOU MUST BE **PROUD**!

PROUD?
AFTER ALL HE'S DONE?
I...DON'T KNOW HOW TO FEEL.
THERE'S STILL **SO MUCH** TO DO.

WE'LL FIGURE IT OUT, DREW.
WE'LL FIX IT.
WHO? JUST YOU AND ME?
BECAUSE NO ONE ELSE IN ART CLUB CAN AGREE ON **ANYTHING**.

HEY, DREW.
HEY, ZEN.
AMEER.
HI.
SO, I, UH...
I WANTED TO **APOLOGIZE**.
FOR STARTING THAT BIG FIGHT WITH DORIAN.
I THOUGHT BEING A HERO MEANT BEATING UP BAD GUYS, AND--
IT MAKES EVERYTHING WORSE, AMEER!
I KNOW. THERE ARE LOTS OF WAYS TO BE A HERO.
I WANT TO TRY A **NEW** WAY.
OH.
IS SOMETHING GOING ON?
DID WE PLAN SOMETHING FOR ART CLUB?
I DON'T HAVE ANYTHING ON MY SCHEDULE!

NO, BECK, WE WERE JUST... CATCHING UP.
SINCE WE HAVEN'T BEEN TALKING MUCH LATELY.
OH.

WITH ALL OUR FIGHTING AND DISAGREEMENTS...
WE HAVEN'T REALLY BEEN MUCH OF A CLUB, HAVE WE?

ARE WE... **OKAY**?
UH...
I MEAN...

WHY DOES EVERYONE LOOK SO **SERIOUS**?
DON'T WE HAVE AN INSTITUTE TO SAVE?

WE--WHAT, DO YOU HAVE A **PLAN**?
YUP.

YOU... YOU FIGURED OUT HOW TO REVERSE YOUR SPELL AND FIX DORIAN?
NOPE, NOT EVEN CLOSE.
SO...
WHAT'S YOUR PLAN?!
TO GET **YOU** TO HELP ME MAKE A PLAN.
WHAT?!
THAT'S NOT A PLAN!!
YOU CALL THAT A **PLAN**?!
IT'S--
CLEARLY, YOU HAVE **A LOT** TO TEACH ME ABOUT PLANS.
I--
ARE YOU FREE AFTER SCHOOL?

CHAPTER 6:
MAKING
PLANS

WOW, BECK, YOUR ROOM IS REALLY--
I KNOW, DON'T EVEN **SAY** IT.

HUH?
SAY **WHAT**?

IT'S A **MESS**.
I WASN'T EXPECTING COMPANY.

UH, YOU THINK **THIS** IS MESSY?
YOU OBVIOUSLY HAVEN'T SHARED A ROOM WITH A SIX-YEAR-OLD.
HA HA, I GUESS NOT.

DID YOU BRING GLOOP?
YEAH.
IF WE CAN REVERSE THE SPELL ON HIM, WE CAN FIX DORIAN, RIGHT?
I HOPE SO. WHAT HAVE YOU LEARNED ABOUT YOUR SPELL?
AT FIRST, I THOUGHT IT WAS TOTALLY **RANDOM**.
BUT I TRIED TO LOOK FOR PATTERNS, MAP IT OUT.
EXCELLENT. THAT DATA WILL BE INVALUABLE.
LET'S SAY THIS WAS GLOOP BEFORE MY SPELL...
HIS DEFAULT STATE.
THE SPELL WARPS HIM IN ALL THESE WEIRD WAYS, BUT...
IT EVENTUALLY CYCLES HIM BACK THROUGH HERE.
FOR JUST A MOMENT.

IF WE TIME IT PERFECTLY, WE CAN STOP IT THE EXACT SECOND HE'S BACK TO NORMAL.
THE MILLISECOND, TJ. WE'LL HAVE TO BE INCREDIBLY PRECISE.
THIS--IT MIGHT NOT BE POSSIBLE.
WELL, IF THERE'S ANYONE WHO CAN FIGURE IT OUT, IT'S YOU, BECK.
I...THANKS.
BUT IT'S GOING TO TAKE TIME TO GET IT RIGHT.
I'M NOT IN A HURRY.
AND...
DORIAN WILL BE SO MUCH MORE COMPLICATED.
HE'S GOING TO FIGHT US THE WHOLE TIME.
IT'LL BE AN ABSOLUTE MESS.
IT'S OKAY, BECK.
LET'S BREAK IT ALL DOWN INTO LITTLE PIECES, RIGHT?
AND THEN PUT THEM BACK TOGETHER, LIKE, UH...
LIKE A BIG, BEAUTIFUL PUZZLE.
RIGHT! LET'S GET STARTED!

THAT EVENING...
IS EVERYONE TUCKED IN?
DO YOU NEED ANY MORE PILLOWS?
OR...?

OH! LEVI!
HOW MANY MORE **ARE** THERE?
AREN'T YOU GETTING **TIRED**?
BECAUSE I AM.

I GUESS I DON'T NEED TO TELL **YOU** THAT.
YOU'VE BEEN **INCREDIBLE** THROUGH ALL THIS, LEVI.
I KNOW YOU'VE MESSED UP AND MADE MISTAKES, BUT...
YOU'VE DONE **SO MUCH** TO MAKE THINGS BETTER FOR EVERYONE ELSE.
IT'S KIND OF AMAZING.
IT'S FUNNY...
I MIGHT HAVE DRAWN **YOU**...
BUT **YOU'RE** THE ONE WHO INSPIRES **ME**.

LATER, AT THE INSTITUTE...

ROARRR

GRRRR
AAA!!
RARR

GRAB
AA!
SMASH!!

BITE BITE BITE

EEEEE!
RARRGH!!
EEE!

MOMENTS LATER, IN DREW'S BEDROOM...
LEVI, YOU'RE BACK ALREADY?
IS EVERYTHING--
EEEE!!

AAA!!!
LEVI!

LEVI!!!

EEE!!!
SMASH!!

RARRGHHH!
EE?
HRRRRRRR

LEVI!!!

LEVI, COME BACK!

WHAT **HAPPENED**?!

PLEASE... **PLEASE** BE OKAY.

I'M WORRIED THAT HE...HE MIGHT BE...

WE'LL HELP!!!

WHAT CAN WE DO??

WE HAVE TO SAVE LEVI!!!!!!

ARE YOU OKAY???

WAHHHHA!

WE HAVE TO DO IT TOMORROW.
ARE WE READY? TO...TAKE ON DORIAN?
•••

BECK, ARE WE READY?

WE WILL BE. FIRST THING TOMORROW.

WE CAN DO IT, DREW!!!

WE'RE HERE FOR YOU!

THANKS, EVERYONE! I...THAT MEANS A LOT.

CHAPTER 7:
REUNITED

I'M GLAD YOU'RE ALL HERE, KIDS, BUT...
WHAT'S YOUR **PLAN**?
FOR DEFEATING DORIAN, SAVING LEVI, AND, WELL...THE ENTIRE INSTITUTE?

WOULD YOU LIKE TO HEAR ALL FORTY-SEVEN STEPS ON OUR AGENDA?
OR JUST THE TOP-LINE ITEMS?
UHH...

WE DON'T ACTUALLY WANT TO **DEFEAT** DORIAN, MR. SCHNEIDER.
WE JUST WANT TO **STOP** HIM, NOT **HURT** HIM.

RIGHT, OF COURSE.
HE'S BEEN THROUGH **A LOT**.
YOU **ALL** HAVE.

WE'VE ALL MADE MISTAKES, DONE SOME THINGS WE REGRET.
THAT'S...JUST WHAT HAPPENS IN A SCARY, STRESSFUL SITUATION.
IT CAN BRING OUT THE WORST IN ANYBODY.

BUT IT CAN ALSO BRING US **BACK TOGETHER**...
AND EVEN BRING OUT THE **BEST** IN US.

DOING SOMETHING **BAD** DOESN'T MAKE YOU A **MONSTER**.
AND SO I'M TRYING **NOT** TO THINK OF **DORIAN** AS ONE.

I...WELL... WONDERFUL!
I'LL CALL CORNELIA AND TELL HER WE'RE ON OUR WAY! WITH A PLAN!
WOULD ANYONE LIKE COOKIES BEFORE WE GO?
OR...SHOULD I PACK SOME FOR THE ROAD?

SOON...
OKAY, SO EVERYONE KNOWS WHAT TO DO?

TJ AND BECK WILL COME WITH ME TO THE CLOUD FORTRESS.
THAT'S WHERE WE'LL MAKE OUR STAND.

AMEER AND I WILL FIND LEVI AND HANNAH.
AND ANYONE ELSE WHO'LL JOIN THE FIGHT!
IT'S GOING TO BE **EPIC**!

HEY, THIS MIGHT BE CORNY, BUT...
LET'S PUT OUR HANDS TOGETHER AND...

ON THREE...
TWO...
ONE...

ART CLUB UNITED!!!

THEY'RE RATHER REMARKABLE, AREN'T THEY?
WOO-HOO!!

YOU MUST BE PROUD.
I AM.
I REALLY, REALLY AM.

NOW...
LET'S JUST **HOPE** THEY KNOW WHAT THEY'RE **DOING**.

INSIDE THE INSTITUTE...
DREW! IN HERE!
DID YOU FIND LEVI?
IS HE...?
HE'S... IN ROUGH SHAPE.
OH MY--
LEVI!!!
WAKE UP!
CAN YOU HEAR ME?!
HURRY, CAP!
WE NEED TO GET HIM OUT OF THERE!

LEVI, LOOK!

LOOK WHO I BROUGHT!

RR?

AWWW!

SO CUTE, AND YET SO GROSS.

RRARRRRGHHHH

AHH!!

HURRY!

WE'VE GOT TO KEEP MOVING!

WOW, ZEN! I HEARD IT WAS **IMPRESSIVE,** BUT...
THIS IS... I DON'T EVEN...
THANKS!

BUT IT'S ALREADY TAKEN SOME HITS.
IS THIS REALLY WHERE WE SHOULD MAKE OUR STAND?
I...
ROARR!!

WAS THAT **DORIAN**?
HE SOUNDS **CLOSE**!
WE-- WE HAVE TO HURRY!

BECK, IT'S **OKAY**.

WE'VE **GOT** THIS.

I-- YOU'RE RIGHT.

OKAY, DEEP BREATH. WE CAN **DO** THIS.

AWWW! YOU'RE FINALLY **GETTING ALONG**!

YOU'VE BOTH COME SO FAR!!

YUP, YAY FOR US.

NOW LET'S SAVE THIS STUPID **INSTITUTE** ALREADY.

HANNAH? WE--

HE'S OKAY, DON'T WORRY!

I HOPE YOU'RE NOT MAD AT US.

OR NOT **TOO** MAD, BECAUSE...

WE NEED YOU! AND EVERYONE ELSE YOU CAN GET!

WE'RE SETTING UP AT THE CLOUD FORTRESS, AND...

YOU **ARE** MAD, AREN'T YOU?

HE'S ALMOST HERE!
CAP TRIED TO DISTRACT HIM, BUT--
AMEER!
I DON'T KNOW IF SHE'S GOING TO HELP US!
HANNAH...
SPEAKING AS A MOTHER, I UNDERSTAND HOW ANGRY YOU MUST BE.
BUT THESE CHILDREN ARE OUR ONLY HOPE OF SAVING YOUR HOME.
PLEASE, HANNAH.
WE NEED TIME FOR OUR PLAN TO WORK. AND WE NEED YOU TO HOLD BACK DORIAN UNTIL WE'RE READY.
RRRARR
MEET US AT THE CLOUD FORTRESS! HURRY!!

HE'S COMING!!
WHAT?!
YOU'RE READY, RIGHT?
ARE YOU **SERIOUS**?!
EVERYTHING HAS TO BE **PERFECTLY CALIBRATED**, DREW.
EXACTLY!
UMMMM, OKAY, WELL... COOL.
BECAUSE... NO RUSH.

WHERE'S HANNAH AND HER ARMY? WE **NEED** THEM!

WAIT, ZEN. MAYBE WE **DON'T.**

WHAT, **CAPTAIN COCKATOO** IS GOING TO TAKE ON DORIAN BY **HIMSELF**?

NO.

MAYBE...

WE **DON'T** HAVE TO FIGHT AT ALL.

HRMM?
THE CAT! THE STATUE!
YOU WERE RIGHT, DREW! THAT'S WHAT HE WANTS!
BUT--
BUT IT'S NOT **READY**!!
IT'S NOT GLUED TOGETHER, AND IT'S GONNA--
TNK KRK

UH-OH.

RARGHH!!

KEEP HIM AWAY FROM OUR EQUIPMENT! PROTECT THE FORTRESS!
WE NEED MORE TIME!!

CAP, YOU KNOW WHAT TO DO!

WAIT, AMEER, DON'T TRY AND--
AND **WHAT**? HE'S TRYING SOMETHING TOTALLY NEW!

GRAB
HRR?

GAHH!!

EVERYONE ELSE, JOIN THE CHAIN IF YOU CAN!
HOLD HIM BACK!
AWWW, AMEER!
YOU REALLY **LISTENED** TO ME!!
YAY FOR LOVE MAGIC!

KIDS! SHE'S HERE!
THEY'RE ALL HERE!
ARE-- ARE WE TOO **LATE**?
NO, NOT AT ALL!
WE NEED TO KEEP DORIAN AWAY FROM OUR EQUIPMENT AND HOLD HIM IN PLACE UNTIL WE--
UNTIL--
GRRAARR!!

ERRR?

RARRR!!!

HOLD HIM STEADY, EVERYONE!!

UNTIL WE GIVE THE SIGNAL!!

LET'S COUNT DOWN TOGETHER, YEAH?
YEAH!

THREE...

TWO...

ONE...

GO!!!

VRMMMMMM

CLEAR THE AREA!
GET AWAY FROM HIM BEFORE--

VKKZZZZ

RR?

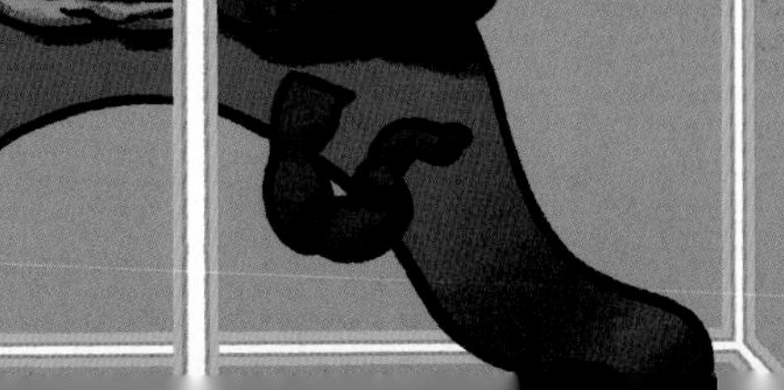

HEY, GUYS? IS THIS THE PLAN?
TO SLICE HIM UP WITH LASERS?
NOT EXACTLY, DREW.
WE'RE HOLDING HIM STILL SO WE CAN WORK ON HIM PIECE BY PIECE.
LIKE AN ENORMOUS, ANGRY PUZZLE.
IT'LL TAKE PERFECT TIMING, BUT IF WE STICK TO THE PLAN...
AND WE'RE LUCKY...
WE MIGHT BE ABLE TO FIX HIM.
ARE YOU READY, BRU? GLOOP?
GLOOP! YOU'RE BACK TO NORMAL!
AND GLOOPIER THAN EVER!
HA HA!

YOU CAN DO IT, TJ!
YOUR MAGIC IS **AMAZING**.
THIS IS GONNA BE AWESOME!
YEAH!

OKAY...
LET'S DO THIS.

SENSOR READINGS ARE GOOD.
CASTING THE SPELL...
NOW!

MY WORD.
I... I DON'T KNOW WHAT TO SAY.
I KNOW. I AM **SO PROUD** OF THESE KIDS RIGHT NOW...
AND A TINY BIT **TERRIFIED** OF THEM.

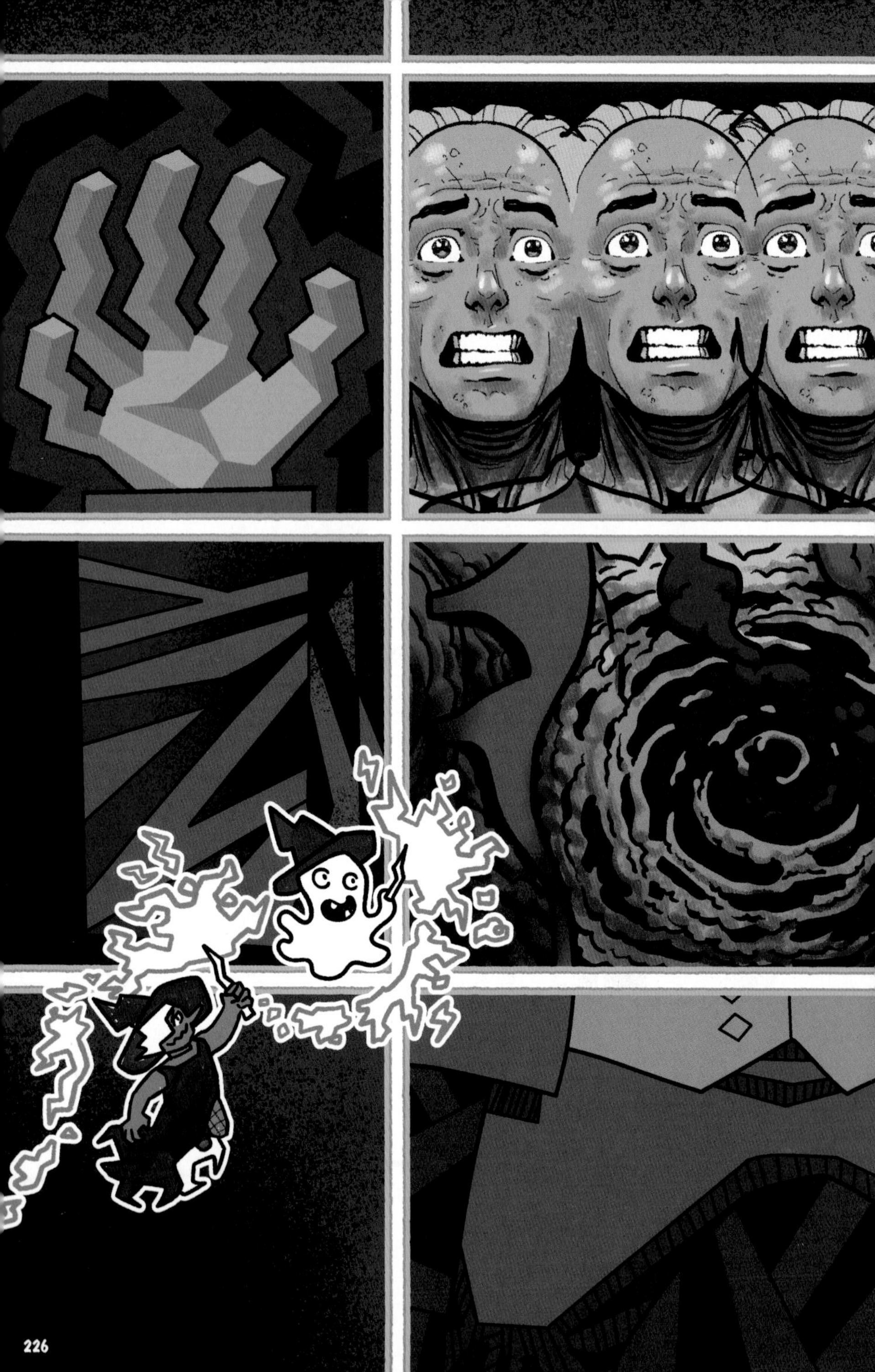

DID IT WORK?
IS...HE OKAY?

LATER THAT DAY...
CORNELIA? WHAT HAPPENS NOW?
I HAVEN'T EVEN FIXED DOODLEVILLE YET.
I CAN'T IMAGINE HOW LONG IT WILL TAKE TO FIX THE **WHOLE INSTITUTE**.
WILL IT HAVE TO STAY CLOSED? **FOREVER**?
NOT FOREVER, DREW.
BUT... FOR NOW.

UNLESS...
DO ANY OF YOUR FRIENDS HAVE SOME KIND OF SPELL THAT CAN MAGICALLY FIX ALL OF THIS?
I CAN CHECK, BUT...I DON'T THINK SO.
THEN I GUESS WE HAVE A LOT OF WORK TO DO, DON'T WE?
WE CAN HELP?
ALL OF US?
BECAUSE I WANT TO!
I HAVE **A LOT** OF IDEAS FOR THIS PLACE!
I'M SURE YOU DO, DREW.
LET'S GET STARTED.

CHAPTER 8: GETTING STARTED

CLOSED
(GRAND REOPENING
COMING...SOON?)

GOOD MORNING, GREG! HOW IS IT IN THERE?
STILL A MESS?

YOU KNOW IT, DREW.

WANT A DONUT?

ABSOLUTELY I DO!

THANKS, DREW!
YOU BET!

HEY, AMEER!
I'VE GOT DONUTS!
STUPENDOUS!

OOH,
I LOVE THESE
ONES!
ME TOO!

OH, DANG.
IT'S OKAY! HERE'S A NAPKIN!

IT LOOKS LIKE HANNAH AND DORIAN ARE GETTING ALONG!
OR AT LEAST... THEY'RE WILLING TO WORK WITH EACH OTHER?
YEAH, MOSTLY.
THEY'VE HAD SOME DIFFERENT IDEAS ABOUT HOW TO DO THINGS, BUT...
DON'T WE ALL?
HA HA, RIGHT!
AWWW! THE PAINTING LOOKS SO EMPTY NOW.
IT LOOKS FINE! NOW COME ON!

HOW LONG WILL IT TAKE TO SET UP THE FORTRESS AGAIN?
NOT LONG.
ARE YOU ADDING ANYTHING NEW?
ARE YOU TAKING SUGGESTIONS?
BECAUSE--
HAHAHAHA!
JUST WAIT AND SEE!
NEW DOOD OPENIN

WELCOME TO
DOODL
THE DOODLE DINER

EVILL

THE DOODLE DINER
HI, THAD!
HI, RICKY!
WHAT'S THE SPECIAL TODAY?
SPAGHETTI WITH BOOGER BALLS!
AND GOOPY GARLIC BREAD!
UH, WOW!
WANT SOME DONUTS?
HOPEFULLY, THERE AREN'T ANY BOOGERS IN THEM, BUT...
THEY'RE STILL GOOD!

SO THIS WILL BE THE NEW **DOODLEVILLE,** DREW?
AN INTERACTIVE EXHIBIT AT THE INSTITUTE?
YEAH!
KIDS CAN ADD THEIR OWN DRAWINGS TO IT.
I'M EXCITED TO SEE WHAT HAPPENS!
BUT...HOW WILL WE MAINTAIN ORDER?
IT COULD SOON DESCEND INTO **TOTAL CHAOS**.
AHA! WELL...
I DREW TWO NEW DOODLES TO KEEP THINGS IN LINE!
WANNA SEE?

I CALL THEM... MR. SCHNOODLE AND KRONGZILLA.
I HOPE YOU'RE NOT UPSET BY HOW THEY LOOK.
THEY JUST... CAME OUT LIKE THAT?
THEY'RE WONDERFUL!
CORNELIA, SHE LOOKS JUST LIKE YOU!
WHAT?!
I--THEY-- IS MY NOSE REALLY THAT BIG?!
IT'S PRETTY BIG, GRAMMY!

WHAT'S GOING ON?
ARE THOSE NEW DOODLES?
HA HA!
AWWW!
LOOK!
YOU KNOW...
I SPENT SO LONG WORRYING ABOUT HOW TO MAKE DOODLEVILLE PERFECT ALL ON MY OWN...
BUT THEN I REALIZED **THAT** WAS THE **PROBLEM**.
I DIDN'T **HAVE** TO DO IT ON MY OWN.
COME TO
IT'S SO MUCH MORE **FUN** LIKE THIS, TOO.
SURE, IT COULD GET CHAOTIC, BUT...
I'M NOT WORRIED.
NO?

WELCOME TO
DOODL

EVILLE
I THINK IT'S GOING TO BE MAGICAL.

THE
END